EA

APPADOCIA

TIGRIS

ASSYRIA

EUPHRATES

SYRIA

PERSIA

2

ARABIA

SEVEN WONDERS
OF THE ANCIENT WORLD

1 The Great Pyramid of Giza

2 The Hanging Gardens of Babylon

3 The Colossus of Rhodes

4 The Mausoleum at Halicarnassus

5 The Temple of Artemis at Ephesus

6 The Statue of Zeus at Olympia

7 The Lighthouse at Alexandria

In memory of Frances Lincoln, friend and publisher
"...how often you and I tired the sun with talking..."
(from a poem by Callimachus). – M.H

First published in Great Britain in 2003 by
Frances Lincoln Limited, 4 Torriano Mews
Torriano Avenue, London NW5 2RZ
www.franceslincoln.com

British Library Cataloguing in Publication Data
available on request

ISBN 0-7112-1986-9

Set in Palatino

Printed in Singapore

1 3 5 7 9 8 6 4 2

SEVEN WONDERS

OF THE ANCIENT WORLD

Mary Hoffman

Illustrated by M.P. Robertson

FRANCES LINCOLN

You may know that there were "Seven Wonders" in the ancient world, but could you name them? They are the Great Pyramid, the Hanging Gardens of Babylon, the Mausoleum at Halicarnassus, the statue of Zeus at Olympia, the Colossus of Rhodes, the Temple of Artemis at Ephesus and the Lighthouse at Alexandria.

It's a strange list: two tombs, two statues, a temple, a lighthouse and a garden, and it wasn't written down in this form until the 16th century – at least, not in any book that survives. The more ancient lists, such as those by Antipater of Sidon and Philo of Byzantium, chose the walls of Babylon as well as its famous "hanging" gardens and did not include the Lighthouse.

But there was a splendid man who lived in Alexandria in the third century BC, who wrote a book of wonders which has not survived. He was Callimachus, a poet who disapproved of long poems, and librarian of the famous library at Alexandria.

I believe that if anyone would have included the Lighthouse in his list it would be Callimachus, who may have watched it being built and certainly could see it every day on his journey to work.

So Callimachus and his book of wonders are real, but I have made up his slave Philip. Their journey takes them to visit five of the Seven Wonders, and the other two are described, at a time around 260 BC, when it was possible to see all seven, if you had time and money and the stamina to make the journey.

The only one you can still see today is the oldest – the Great Pyramid at Giza, where I myself have stood and wondered. But with a bit of imagination, we can make the journey with Philip and his master and enjoy all seven of the sights that have come to be known as Wonders of the World.

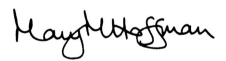

It was a cold spring morning when my master woke me early. "Get up, Philip, and wash your face! We are going on a journey to see marvels!"

I was still half asleep as I packed my master's things. He's always full of surprises, a good master, even if he loses his temper quite easily.

It's not a bad life working for a librarian, even though he sometimes forgets that he's not a schoolmaster any more and treats me like one of his old pupils instead of his slave.

"Where are we going, master?" I dared to ask at last.

"Why, everywhere!" said Callimachus, in a great good humour. "It's time I got away from the library and the museum – all those scholars buzzing around like flies on a goat-herd! We are going to see the wonders of the world and I shall write a book about them."

"Where are we going first?" I asked. "And why does it have to be so early?'

"We are going to Giza," said my master. "Now, stop yawning, Philip. We need to catch a boat going up the Nile."

The Nile! Everyone in Alexandria knows that our country depends on that mighty river, but I had never travelled on it.

Now we boarded a boat and put our lives in the hands of the strong sailors rowing upstream. I clung on to the side all the way and watched the crocodiles in the water. We were very hungry indeed by the time the boat pulled in at a landing-stage and let us off.

But there was no rest for us. We staggered on wobbly legs, but my master bargained with a local man for two camels and we set off over the sand.

I don't know which is worse, being on a boat or sitting on a camel!

10

We rode for what felt
like hours and then we saw it
on the horizon, a huge mountain
with completely smooth sides.
"What is it, master?" I cried.
"Your first wonder, Philip," said Callimachus,
"and the oldest you will see. That is the great tomb of
King Cheops – the Pyramid, they call it – and it is already
more than two thousand years old."
It looked to me as if it would last at least another two thousand years.
I had never seen anything so enormous. As we got closer, it got bigger and
bigger and we saw that there were two other pyramids behind it.
It was like a mountain range, but my master assured me that it had been
built by humans, not formed by nature. "Hundreds of thousands of men, Philip,
and hundreds of thousands of blocks of granite under that smooth surface."
We were greeted by a priest of the temple of Cheops who seemed to know
Callimachus, and I was very glad to hear him say that a meal was waiting for us.

Our journey back down the Nile seemed more natural, with the wind in our sails. I felt I had already travelled enough for a lifetime, but as soon as we reached the harbour at Alexandria, Callimachus bustled us on to a much bigger ship. It was a trading ship taking grain to Greece.

"Where are we going now, master?" I asked, in some fear, as the ship's planks heaved underneath me.

"To an island and another wonder," was all he would say.

There were several other passengers on the trip and one was a perfume merchant who had travelled the world. He and my master were soon firm friends and swapped tales of sights they had seen.

I was feeling very unwell with the movement of the sea and my master brought me a cup of wine.

"You must come and hear this merchant, Philip," he said kindly. "He is going to tell us about another wonder – too far away for us to visit, though I'd love to include it in my book."

So I staggered up on deck, and there was the merchant with quite a circle of people around him.

"Carry on," said Callimachus. "Tell us everything you have seen of the Hanging Gardens."

"Babylon..." said the merchant. "The most beautiful city in the world. Who hasn't heard of its blue walls with their lions, bulls and dragons?"

I kept very quiet, since I for one hadn't heard of them. But the merchant went on, "In the walls are a hundred gates of brass leading to streets which criss-cross the city in straight lines. The river Euphrates runs through it and on its west bank stands the palace built by Nebuchadnezzar. And that is where the hanging gardens are.

The water runs uphill and the terraces reach as high as the palace walls. They are filled with every kind of plant – acacia, cypress, juniper, tamarisk, myrtle, pomegranate, fig, olive..."

On and on went the list, until my eyelids drooped. I slept and dreamed of a garden floating in the air.

I woke with a jolt, back in my own bunk, and wondered if I had dreamed the story of a garden where the water ran uphill. But there was no time to think about it now. My master was calling us up on deck.

"Come, or you'll miss the best view of our third wonder!"

As we sailed towards an island, the dawn broke and I could see a massive figure standing in its harbour. I was terrified. No mortal man could be so huge!

"Master, is it a monster?" I cried.

"No, it is the great god Helios, lord of the rising sun," said Callimachus. "Can you see the rays of the sun round his head?"

Closer and closer we sailed, and it was a long time before I realised that what we were seeing was a great bronze statue which gleamed like gold in the sunrise. It towered over us as we moored; its very ankles were taller than me. It was indeed a wonder.

We stayed on the island, which was called Rhodes, long enough for Callimachus to make some notes, then we left the harbour and its gigantic guardian behind and sailed north-west round some smaller islands.

My master was in a very good mood. "I have gathered material for three of the Seven Wonders I'm going to put in my book," he said. "And now we're about to see the fourth. Our great king, Alexander himself, saw it when it was only about twenty years old – that was over a hundred years ago."

But he wouldn't tell us what it was. We sailed on up the coast of Caria until we came to another harbour. No god loomed over this one, but a tall white building covered in figures.

"Halicarnassus," said my master, "and that is the tomb of its king – Mausollus."

"A tomb?" I said, "but look how tall it is!"

"Wasn't the pyramid even taller?" replied Callimachus. "And look, this one has a little pyramid at the top."

And so it did. Only it didn't come to a point, but stopped short at a flat platform on which there was a marble charioteer, with four white horses to pull his chariot.

"King Mausollus himself," said Callimachus. "And this wonder was built by his loving wife, who was also his sister."

We stayed in Halicarnassus a week, then suddenly we were off again in another trading ship, following our north-west course. I was quite a good sailor by now and was up on deck when we next headed towards land, on the coast of Lydia.

"Now we are going to see the most beautiful temple in the world," said Callimachus, "as full of white pillars as a forest is of green trees."

"Whose temple is it, master?" I asked.

"Artemis, the huntress," he said. "Apollo's sister, who never married. But in Ephesus, where we are going, she is worshipped as the Mother Goddess – you'll see."

And I did. The temple was just as marvellous as my master said. Some of the pillars had whole stories pictured round their bases and my master forgot he wasn't a school teacher any more and told me the stories for days.

The statue of Artemis showed her to be a true mother to the people of Ephesus. It had more breasts than a sow with a dozen piglets to feed and the local people had hung offerings of fruit and flowers all over it. Callimachus bought a little silver model of the statue from a merchant in front of the temple.

"This will remind me of the lady Artemis when I'm back in the library writing my book," he said.

When we next boarded a ship, we sailed south-east, passing Halicarnassus and Rhodes again. And my master sat me down beside him on the deck for another lesson.

"Our sixth wonder is too far for us to visit on this voyage," he said. "But I saw it when I was a young man, studying in Athens. It is about three hundred miles to our west, at Olympia."

"Is it to do with the games?" I asked.

"In a way," said Callimachus. "It is the statue of the father of the gods himself, great king Zeus, in whose honour the games are held. Of course it had to be the grandest ever made, since it shows the greatest god. So they got the best sculptor of the day – this was over two hundred years ago – called Pheidias."

"There's a copy of his statue of Athene back home in Alexandria," I said.

"Well, his Zeus had to be even better than that," said Callimachus. "He showed the great god seated on a throne of ebony and jewels. The god himself has skin of ivory and robes of gold; he is forty feet high, with his head almost grazing the ceiling of the temple. The goddess of Victory perches on his right hand and his left holds the eagle-headed sceptre.

And in front of the statue, to reflect the sunlight coming through a high window in the temple, is a pool of olive oil, five inches deep, which is always kept filled, so that the light sparkles off mighty Zeus' robes."

I sat in silence on the deck, imagining the statue. I felt I could see it in my mind's eye.

As the days wore on, I realised we were sailing back to Alexandria. I know Callimachus can be a bit absent-minded, so I had to say something.

"Master, we have seen or heard of only six wonders and yet we seem to be on our way home. Have you forgotten the seventh?"

"No, Philip," he said, "but I'm glad to hear you have been paying attention. The Great Pyramid, the Hanging Gardens, the Colossus, the Mausoleum, the Temple of Artemis, the Statue of Zeus – they do indeed add up only to six. But the seventh wonder is to be a surprise."

It was getting dark when we glimpsed the coast of Egypt. I thought we would weigh anchor and wait for dawn to make our return home. But in the pitch dark a dazzling light suddenly blazed out.

"There it is," said my master's voice softly in my ear. "Our seventh wonder – the lighthouse of our own city!"

I couldn't believe it. We had a wonder of our own in Alexandria, worthy to be named alongside all the other marvels we had seen! And yet I have known that lighthouse all my life. You can almost see it from the library.

"I remember it being built," said Callimachus. "It took fifteen years. Sostratus made it and dedicated it to the saviour gods Castor and Pollux, who protect sailors. It has shone out over the Mediterranean for over twenty years, saving lives."

We sailed slowly and safely towards home, our path lit by our final wonder. I knew that after all I had seen and heard, I would look at everything with new eyes. My master's book might be about only seven marvels, but for me, for the rest of my life, I would see wonders wherever I went.

Callimachus (about 310-235 BC)

He was an ordinary schoolmaster, teaching grammar in a suburb of Alexandria, until he was introduced to the king, Ptolemy II (Philadelphus). He probably became librarian in 255 BC and continued in that job for the next twenty years. He wrote over 800 books, very few of which have survived. He says in one of his poems that he never travelled on the water, but we can take this with a pinch of sea-salt, because he was born in Cyrene (in present-day Libya) and educated in Athens and must have sailed from there to Alexandria. It is also reasonable to deduce that he had seen the statue of Zeus, from a fragment of a poem he wrote to a friend who was going to visit Olympia.

The Great Pyramid of Giza - pages 12-13

This was built as a tomb for King Khufu (Cheops) about 2560 BC. It still stands, with the pyramids of Khafra (Chephren) and Menkaure (Mykerinus) in the desert in Giza, which is now a suburb of Cairo. No-one knows exactly how long it took to build or how many men and blocks of stone were involved. But, given the tools that the ancient Egyptians had, it represents a marvel of engineering and architecture which has never been surpassed. It would have already been well over 2,000 years old when Callimachus and Philip saw it.

The Hanging Gardens of Babylon – pages 16-17

The city of Babylon still exists in what is now Iraq. In the ancient world it was the powerful capital of a mighty civilisation and one of its most famous kings was Nebuchadnezzar II (604-562 BC). He was the one who, in the Book of Daniel, captured the Jews and threw Shadrach, Meshach and Abednego into a fiery furnace. Legend tells that he built the magnificent gardens for his queen Amytis, because she was homesick for the mountains of her homeland. But no evidence of any such gardens has been found at Babylon and some scholars think that they have been confused with the gardens built by Sennacherib at Nineveh, about 200 miles further north.

The Colossus of Rhodes – pages 18-19

This gigantic statue of the sun-god Helios was built near the harbour on the Greek island of Rhodes between 294 and 282 BC. Cast in sections in bronze by the sculptor Chares, it stood 34 metres high. But it could not have stood astride the harbour mouth, because no engineering could have spanned the 400-metre gap in that way. It was destroyed by an earthquake in 226 BC, which broke the statue at the knees, but the fallen figure remained on Rhodes for nearly 900 years until it was sold as scrap metal by the Arabs in the 7th century AD. No trace of it or its site remains.

The Mausoleum at Halicarnassus – pages 20-21

King Mausollus reigned from 377-353 BC in Caria and had such a magnificent tomb and monument built for himself (completed about 350 BC) that the word "mausoleum" entered the language to describe any grand tomb. It collapsed in the 13th century AD and some remains of the structure were built into the castle of St Peter at Bodrum (ancient Halicarnassus) in Turkey. But excavations in the mid-19th century found more pieces, including what may be the statue of Mausollus himself, which are now in the British Museum.

The Temple of Artemis at Ephesus – pages 22-23

There were several versions of this building in what is now Turkey. It was first built with money supplied by the famously rich Croesus in the 6th century BC and burnt down by Herostratus in 356 BC. Along came Alexander the Great in 334 BC and offered to pay for the reconstruction, but was turned down. The people of Ephesus rebuilt their beloved temple so successfully that it soon became acknowledged as one of the wonders of the world. (You can see some fragments of it in the British Museum, including one of the sculpted column bases.)

The Statue of Zeus at Olympia – pages 24-27

A new temple to Zeus at Olympia was completed in 456 BC and the huge statue of the god was begun by the sculptor Pheidias in 438 BC. It was made of gold and ivory, seated on an ebony throne, and was 13 metres tall, its head almost touching the temple ceiling. Olympia was the site of the Olympic Games, which began as part of a festival celebrating Zeus, the chief of the Greek gods. Nothing remains of the statue, which was taken to Byzantium and later destroyed in a fire in about 425 AD. But some fragments of Pheidias' workshop have been discovered at Olympia. Some of what we know of the statue's dimensions comes from a description by Pausanias, who travelled in Greece in the 2nd century AD.

The Lighthouse at Alexandria – pages 30-31

The lighthouse was probably begun in 297 BC, under the reign of the first King Ptolemy. But it wasn't finished until shortly after his son, Ptolemy II came to the throne in 284 BC. It was built on an island called Pharos, which was joined to the mainland by an artificial causeway. The lighthouse itself became known as the Pharos and gave that name to many other lighthouses in the world. It had a statue of Zeus Soter ("Saviour") at the top. By the time of its destruction in 1303 AD the statue of Zeus had been replaced by a domed Islamic mosque with the crescent symbol at the top. Some of the stones from the original lighthouse have been built into the wall of the Qait Bey fortress which stands on its site in Alexandria.

BLAC

THRACE

MACEDONIA

LYDIA

5

4

3

AEGEAN SEA

6

MEDITERRANEAN
SEA

7

1

EGYPT

NILE

LIBYA